FLY AWAY HOME

FLY AWAY HOME

written by
STEVEN BRET BRENEMAN
illustrated by
CAROL JOY

BellwoodPress
Evanston, Illinois

Bellwood Press, P.O. Box 605, Evanston, IL 60204-0605

Library of Congress Cataloging in Publication Data

Breneman, Steven Bret, 1943–
  Fly away home.

  Summary: A sparrow and a ladybug determine to reach
the beautiful garden on top of Emerald Hill despite the
barrier formed by a cadre of unfriendly crows under the
leadership of a crafty parrot.
  [1. Birds—Fiction. 2. Ladybugs—Fiction. 3. Friendship—Fiction]. I. Joy, Carol, 1957– ill. II. Title.
PZ7.B7513Fl 1984   [Fic]   84-6252
ISBN 0-87743-183-3 (soft)

Design by John Solarz

For Eva and Reed

FLY AWAY HOME

*Lo, the Nightingale of Paradise singeth
upon the twigs of the Tree of Eternity,
with holy and sweet melodies. . . .*

—Bahá'u'lláh

1

"There's a ladybug on your arm, Eva!" the little tow-headed boy said. He and his sister sat in the sun beside their pool. Their taffy-colored cocker spaniel, wagging his tail eagerly over a ball beside the boy's feet, looked up at him. The boy picked up the ball and threw it again onto their lawn. Startled by the gesture, a blue jay rose out of the grass, flapped over the rambling garden that spread from the far edge of the lawn, and disappeared into the side of a thickly wooded hill.

The girl watched the orange, yellow, and black shining bead crawl into the hollow of her elbow. "Look! Isn't it pretty, Reed? Granny Cross would love it," she said.

Just then the ladybug flew off her arm and whirred away.

"There it goes!" Reed cried.

"Ladybug, ladybug, fly away home," Eva said quickly with a smile as if the words were the magic the cute little insect would need.

"I'm not even a lady," Lorne, the ladybug, thought to himself, wishing he could somehow communicate with Eva and Reed. "And why do people always think it's time for us to go home? I just got here."

Nevertheless, Lorne did not like the look of that romping dog and headed for the garden where his family was and where most of his friends were playing.

As he entered the blur of colors and the sweet blend of flower-smells that was home, he glimpsed Emerald Hill looming above it. He hoped the crows had not entered the garden yet today. They liked to boss everybody around. The friendly doves and cheerful sparrows usually flew away when the crows arrived. And the ladybugs did their best to look like a piece of leaf or flower and were not free to fly around as much. It was not that the crows liked to eat them. In fact, they joked about how awful ladybugs tasted. The main problem was that the crows liked to play a game in which they caught ladybugs in mid-air with their beaks and tossed them back and forth like colorful beach balls. If one got squashed during the game, it did not bother them very much. They could always catch another.

Lorne landed on a blade of grass that swayed pleasantly for a moment with the weight of his arrival. Other blades of grass bent at different angles as far as he could see, each one a welcome landing place and launching pad for him and his friends. He thought he glimpsed the orange glow of Larry off in the distance under the flowering dogwood tree. There was a rush of wind and a whir of wings, and Loralei landed on the blade beside him. She was a yellow ladybug with black polkadots, and she liked to follow him around. He thought she was nice, but she made him a bit uncomfortable.

"Hi, Lorne," she said cheerily in her musical voice.

"Good-bye," he said and flew off to find Larry.

His friend was bouncing on a blade of grass. The tip of the blade would almost reach the ground, and Larry would disappear in the jungle of grass for an instant and then come swooping back up. Lorne settled onto a blade and watched him.

As Larry reappeared, he called in an excited voice, "Hey, Lornie!" Then he disappeared again. When he came back up, he shouted, "This is fun!" Down he went again. And up again. "Watch this!" Down again. When he swung back up, this time he let go. Lorne saw a blaze of orange and black flash into the air—and his friend was gone.

Lorne looked around for a minute but did not see him.

"Peekaboo!"

Lorne looked up to see Larry peering over the edge of a young dogwood leaf high above him.

"Pretty good, huh?" Larry called.

"Yeah, that was terrific," Lorne said.

"I hardly used my wings at all!"

Lorne knew he was exaggerating, but he pretended to be impressed. It was a good trick whether he used his wings or not.

"Let's go see Spenser," Lorne called. Spenser the Sparrow always had great stories to tell of things he had seen on his flights—and things he had imagined he saw.

"Right! Here I come!" Larry disappeared onto the top of the gently swaying leaf. Lorne knew he was going to do his rolling trick. Larry came tumbling off the lip of the leaf like a painted beebee. He free-fell, spinning slower and slower. Then he opened his bright wings as he plummeted toward Lorne, who had seen and done this many times before. As if an invisible thread suddenly pulled taut, Larry swooped up, hovered like a helicopter, did a firefly flourish in the air, and finally bobbed beside Lorne on his favorite blade for the day.

"Pretty fancy, all right," Lorne said. "You're getting good."

"Spenser's is it?" Larry panted proudly. "What are we waiting for?"

"Guess," Lorne said. "Shall we go then? I'll try your launching trick."

Together they got their blades to bob, then to swing and spring, and then they shot like strokes of watercolor into the fragrant garden air. In his propulsion Lorne narrowly missed another ladybug that was passing.

"Watch it!" he heard Lester yell. He was another one of their friends.

When Lorne's momentum had spent itself, he opened his wings, hovered on a shelf of air, and looked back down toward Lester.

"Hey, Les!" he called. "We're going to see Spenser. Do you want to come?"

"Wait!" came the squeaking voice of this friend he liked so much. Lester made a game upward arc and was soon hovering beside Lorne.

"Let's go!" Larry called from a mulberry twig.

They joined him on the little branch, where the three of them made a decorative line for a moment—orange and black drops of porcelain on the knotty gray-brown bark.

It was spring, and the whole garden was bustling with happy new life. The birds sung a loose and widespread symphony. The different songs of the different birds did not clash but fit together in an effortless, unplanned harmony. The sparrows chirped in cozy, intimate tones. The majestic mourning doves cooed and warbled distantly, as if from the edge of sleep—or from the edge of the world; they seemed to hearken from a higher garden and to be sad to be away from it. The larks sang as brilliantly as they flew, bubbling limpid songs of hope and pristine promise. When the cuckoo sang, it was as if doors opened in the air and a secret fairyland of pastel hues and sprightly forest folk were disclosed.

Sometimes—on certain lucky days—a nightingale could be heard. The life of the garden was suspended then in a trance of enchantment. The song came pouring from high on Emerald Hill, a rush of song that almost ached with beauty.

When it was over, and the last golden note poured from the hillside forest and thinned like hammered gold into the

6

air, grew transparent, and disappeared, everybody was silent for a few minutes and did not know exactly what to do. Should they cry for love and beauty lost? Should they laugh and celebrate for the coming of that joyous song? Should they flee to the magic hillside, seek the hidden nightingale, and beg it to sing again, to always sing, forever and ever?

But the spell always passed, and the life of the garden resumed, almost as before, but completely changed: the colors brighter and more glowing, the scents sweeter and more inspiring—and the bird songs more poignant and ecstatic than they had been before.

A parrot in the garden, who had escaped from his human owners, tried to imitate the song of the nightingale. Often after the last stirring note had faded, there would come the false echo of the parrot's imitation. If you had not just heard the nightingale, you would almost be convinced that it was a nightingale singing. But it was a plastic version of something real.

It always gave Lorne a sick feeling to hear it and made him indignant. It seemed like a mockery. And when the parrot would sing by itself, stirring hopes for a moment that it was the nightingale, Lorne felt crushed to realize that it was the parrot practicing his imitation. Lorne could not understand why some of the ladybugs in the garden, and even some of the birds, said that they thought the parrot sounded exactly like the nightingale. In fact, it amazed him.

For some reason the crows guarded the magic hill from whence the entrancing song came. They would not let anybody go onto that hill, if they could help it. Some people said the crows were following the orders of the nightingale, that they were protectors of the sacred ground. A few said that they were enemies of the nightingale and did not want the people of the garden to come under his wonderful spell. Lorne did not know what to think. Most people thought they were protectors, but he tended to think they were enemies. If the nightingale was anything like his song, the crows were complete opposites. Sometimes Lorne dreamed of sneaking up to Emerald Hill. But when he heard the croakings of the crows, saw their strong beaks and glaring eyes, he thought better of it. He wished that someday the nightingale would come to their garden and sing to them of everything he knew.

2

The three young ladybugs found Spenser in his red maple tree, perched beside the nest of twigs and straw where his wife sat on two little white eggs. The climb was a long one, and they went up the tree in stages, stopping off on the trunk in the dim light two or three times before they reached his branch. They crawled out onto it in high spirits, looking colorful and bright in the cranberry glow of the maple aura. Spenser was fitting a new piece of straw into the side of the nest when they arrived.

As the sparrow pushed the golden-colored needle of straw into place, Lorne flew up to the rim of the nest just above Spenser's eye level.

"Hi, Spenser!" he called, using his yelling voice.

Spenser was not able to speak at first, but he nodded, shaking the nest a little.

"Be careful, honey," his wife said from inside the nest. "You'll spill us all out of here. Oh, hello, Lorne. How nice to see you."

"Morning, ma'am. Is everything coming along all right?"

"If it's the little ones you're referring to, yes, thanks. It won't be long now."

Lester and Larry flew up on either side of Lorne, and the three of them adorned the brown and gold nest like beads. It gave Spenser's wife a lift to see them since she had so little entertainment these days. She only knew about the life of the garden from what Spenser told her—and you had to weed the fact from the fiction from *his* narrative. Sometimes he told her the most amazing things. But she never had the heart to question his tales—he was so sincere.

"Good morning, boys," Spenser said. "The three laddy-bugs. Mind if I call you that?"

There was a tiny, shrill chorus of approval from the colorful guests.

The little brown and cream-colored bird with the shining eyes looked warm and soft in the dimness of the maple shade. Spenser was great. He never made them feel small.

"Many crows down there today?" he asked.

"I didn't see any," Lorne said.

"Uh oh, trouble. They're off planning something."

"I saw a couple by the apple trees," Lester said. "They were picking on a poor young dove. They said he flew too high."

"I've heard that before. But maybe it's a good sign. Maybe they're not plotting something."

"Why are they always so mean?" Larry piped up somewhat angrily.

"Good question," Spenser said, "and I am not sure I can answer it, but maybe there are some nice ones somewhere."

They all reluctantly agreed, as if that were the last word.

Then they heard it. It was the first time in weeks.

"Quiet!" Spenser's wife said. "Listen!"

Pealing through the trees and leaves came the luscious, liquid notes of the nightingale. The song was faint and far off, but the sound seemed strangely close, like a thought, or a feeling in the heart. As rays of sunlight, it poured through the garden, and all else was still and quiet, enchanted by the wondrous song. All love and joy and beauty seemed to vibrate on the air.

Then suddenly there was a loud clamor, a rude croaking from closer by that all but drowned the nightingale's song. Still it penetrated the ugly wall of noise, but the pure rapture of the moment was mixed with a feeling of hopelessness and anger. Those blasted crows! They sure spoiled things.

The glorious song faded on the hushed air. The clamor of the crows, made by the croaking of dozens of them, sounded louder, as if in victory, and then gradually stopped with last ratchety, guttural bursts of pride and perversity.

"That's what they were planning," Spenser said.

"How did they know the nightingale was going to sing this morning?" Lorne asked. He flew to a twig that was right beside Spenser's head.

"They have ways of finding out. They're clever devils, I'll say that, even if they can't tell a man from a mannequin."

"How, Spenser?" Lorne asked earnestly. He loved to talk about the magic hill. "Do they spy on the nightingale and his family?"

"I really don't know very much about it," the sparrow said remotely, poking at a twig in the side of the nest and then looking sharply at Lorne. "There are many mysteries about that garden."

"Garden? Is there a garden on Emerald Hill?"

Spenser felt he had already said too much. This young laddy-bug was too interested in the magic hill. It was not healthy—but he had to admit it was touching.

"Yes, there's a garden up there," he said with a little sigh of resignation. He felt he was getting a foretaste of what it was going to be like to be a parent. He was glad he would only be the father. How much was it okay to tell? He had almost given up talking to his wife about it because she did not really believe him when he told her what he had seen. He could not stand that humoring tone she used, but he understood her disbelief. He would not have believed it either if he had not seen it himself.

3

"Do the crows go into the garden on Emerald Hill?" Lorne asked earnestly.

"How should I know?" Spenser said, trying one last time to defend himself against the laddy-bug's interest. But he felt the sweet fire the high garden aroused in him begin to spread through him and realized that at long last he had found someone who would listen to him and believe him.

Larry and Lester, having come so high in the maple tree, were interested in going even farther and whirred up to the next main branch. Action engrossed them more than conversation.

"But, but . . . ," Lorne said, disappointed and confused. "Spenser, remember that day you told me about the flamingos up there—the big orange-pink birds we thought were only in stories?"

"Yes," Spenser said, yielding to the delightful memory.

"You seemed to know a lot about the magic hill then."

Spenser looked around quickly in that perky, jerky way sparrows have and said, "Look, Lorne, what I'm going to tell you is a secret. Don't tell it to anybody unless they are your very close friends and they really want to know." Spenser had just discovered this rule himself, following a feeling he had. "Come up to my shoulder," he said.

Lorne was surprised and delighted at this invitation. It was a rare treat to ride on a bird. He rose off the twig with a slow, gentle leap and landed lightly in the soft, snuggly down of Spenser's shoulder.

"We'll go where we won't be disturbed," Spenser said. "Honey," he called to his wife with formal affection. "We'll be back in half an hour or so. Please tell Lester and Larry to wait. Or they can go play somewhere if they want to. Lorne and I are going for a little ride."

"All right, Spenser, dear," his wife said with maternal preoccupation, with that mysterious tone she had these days from having secret knowledge of the inside of her eggs. "Mind the crows."

"Get between my wings at the base of my neck," Spenser said. "That's it. Get down a little farther into the feathers. There you go." And they were off.

Spenser tried to keep his flight as smooth and unsparrowlike as possible. Lorne felt like the whole world was rushing at him in a big wind. But soon he was used to the speed and power and peeked out above the brown feathers where he was nestled. Everything looked so grand from up here. The garden paths made a pattern in the trees and shrubbery and flowers. The central birdbath glittered with the splashing of a bird he could not identify. But he could see two crows stalking around it as if on sentry duty.

The little sparrow flying with the ladybug on its brown neck looked special indeed to anyone who might have noticed its bright little burden. Spenser seemed adorned for a rare and formal occasion.

He headed for the copse of willows by the south pond. It was usually quiet and peaceful there—a nice place to talk about the magic hill.

As they arrived, he saw the little tow-headed boy fishing from the big rock. But that was all right. He never hurt anything—except the fish. And the crows hated people. It was good the boy was here.

They landed in the biggest willow, beside a pine tree. Lorne came out onto Spenser's shoulder, letting his breath out with a certain relief. He was blinded for a minute by the silver reflection from the pond. But then he made out the figure of the boy sitting directly across from them in jeans and a red shirt and trailing his float slowly back and forth. He could see one taffy-colored ear of the dog where he lay faithfully beside the rock.

"What other kinds of birds did you see up there?" Lorne asked abruptly.

"He doesn't let up," the sparrow thought. "Quite an appetite." To Lorne he said, "You're really interested in that hill, aren't you?"

"Yes, I guess so." Lorne had not thought about his interest, but he always thought about the magic hill. "I love that song. It's so beautiful—and so important, somehow."

"Yes," the sparrow said. "Let's see. You want to know what kinds of birds I've seen up there?"

"I want to know about the nightingale most," Lorne said a little shyly.

"Okay, but you know I really know very little."

"Will you tell me what you know?"

"Yes, I will."

The ripples from the boy's green float spread continually toward them, and the sun gleamed off his golden head. He had caught a big one last week and was learning to be patient.

"The nightingale is a prisoner," Spenser said.

Lorne felt he had been struck by a heavy blow when he heard these words. The *nightingale* a *prisoner?* The words did not seem to go together. They were opposites. When Lorne heard that celestial song, it always made him think that the nightingale was the only creature that was not a prisoner.

"You mean? . . ."

"The crows. They keep him in the garden. Or try to."

"You mean he gets out sometimes?"

"I mean . . . he gets out whenever he wants to. I'm convinced of it!"

Spenser, caught up in the importance of the topic, spoke now almost as to a peer.

"People have seen him down here. He has always solved their problems, but they never guess that the bird they saw is the one that sings so beautifully. They glimpse him through the leaves like a passing thought or a dream. I think I've seen him once or twice myself."

The fact that the nightingale could be near them at any moment without their knowing it was too much for Lorne to grasp. He knew he must go one step at a time. So he returned to the subject of Emerald Hill.

"Do the crows go into his garden?"

"That's a funny thing. I don't know very much, as I say, but they don't seem to go into the garden very often. They stay on the edge and guard against anybody's going out or coming in. I've only seen crows in there a couple of times, and it's strange—they look embarrassed. Of course, they're completely out of place in such a lovely spot. But they act almost humble when they're in the garden, if you can imagine it, as if they were about to admit the error of their ways, apologize to the nightingale, and let him go."

"How do you get past the crows?"

The sparrow's chest swelled slightly, and his feathers ruffled; but then, remembering a certain note in the nightingale's song, he quickly deflated himself for some reason.

"I go on the nights the crows have their secret ceremonies. They eat a special berry that gets them drunk. Then it's easy to get by them. I have a copy of their calendar, you see, so I know when their vigilance will relax. On those nights they think they're the kings of the world and can do no wrong and aren't so careful."

16

Just then there was a rustling of wings in the pine tree behind them. Spenser looked around quickly and saw a flash of blue. Blue jay. The big bird flapped out of the tree and soared away.

"Uh oh," Spenser thought. "Trouble."

4

Lorne just could not stay away from Spenser. After all of the intriguing tales he had heard the day before, he felt drawn as if by a magnet back to the warm nest in the maple tree.

But as he bobbed and whirred through the air toward the noble tree, he felt that something was wrong. He must have heard Spenser's wife sobbing before he knew it—and before he saw the two eggs splashed out on the grass beneath the tree.

He could not believe his eyes. He did not want to believe that these were Spenser's babies, crushed to death before they even had a chance to live. Had they fallen out of the nest? What had happened?

His first thought, when he heard the sobbing, was to rush to help, but his second was that maybe he should not intrude during such a private, and terrible, moment. But he could not stay away and made his gradual ascent to Spenser's nest.

As soon as he got there, the full force of the nightmare struck him. The nest was trembling with the bereft mother's racking sobs. And Spenser huddled on the branch, his head sunk down between his shoulders. His right wing stuck out at an ugly angle. It was broken.

The crows had come.

Lorne stayed by the trunk of the tree and wept quietly. Just as he would get some control over himself, he would look up and see that tragic scene and start to cry again. Their babies were dead.

He felt a surge of hatred and rage toward the evil crows and went dizzy with the emotions as if *he* had fallen out of the tree.

Right then, seeming to know of the sorrow that had come into the sparrows' lives, the far-off nightingale began to sing. The melody seemed louder and closer. It was penetratingly sweet and uplifting. It was deeply refreshing. It was the precise remedy for dejection and despair. It was pure compassion.

Lorne felt his anger and hatred drop off him like a cloak. He saw Spenser begin to stir, his head emerging by degrees from its miserable hiding place. The sobbing stopped, and the nest became still and quiet again.

But then there was the rushing clamor of the crows, like the cruel clashing of swords. Caught off guard, they rushed to make up for the delay in their defense by cawing and ratcheting more noisily than ever. Nevertheless, the nightingale's song pierced their fierce armor with lofty ease. As the nightingale sang, the pall of grief lifted off the sparrows and their brilliant little friend, and they could hope again.

"They came right before dawn," Spenser explained to Lorne. "I had just started to sing my morning prayers when, without warning, the darkness seemed to get darker, and they fell upon us. There were five of them, I think. They got the calendar."

Spenser was looking more like his old self again. But his wing was broken, and he could not fly. And his fledglings were gone. Nothing could change that.

Suddenly, a terrible thought struck Lorne, as if he, too, were being attacked by the crows. If he had not asked so many questions the day before, it would not have happened! It was his fault that the baby birds were dead just as surely as if he had killed them himself. He was filled with guilt and despair. He felt like shriveling up into nothingness.

"Spenser," he said. "I'm so sorry. It's my fault, I think. Can you ever forgive me? They wouldn't have come if I hadn't made you tell me about the nightingale."

"No, Lorne. Those are dark thoughts. Don't think like that . . . I was a marked bird, you see. They would have slapped me down sooner or later. It helps me to be able to share all of this with someone."

"But it doesn't help me!" Spenser's wife said sharply between quiet sobs. "My babies are gone—dashed away like something worthless! You see, Spenser? You never understood the danger. And now it's too late."

Spenser knew he had to meet his wife's desperate need and to help her get through this terrible time when the very meaning of her life had been cruelly undermined.

"Excuse me, Lorne," he said quietly, with a shade of despair. "Please come back later this evening. Your friendship is very important to me now. It's almost the only thing I have."

And with that the broken-winged sparrow hopped stiffly along the branch to his nest. Lorne started to turn away to go, but something stopped him. Something in the feeble awkwardness of Spenser's movements alarmed him and compelled him to stay until his friend got into his nest.

"Spenser?" the female sparrow's thin, desperate voice said.

"Coming, honey."

The rim of the nest was about three inches above his head. He would have to try to hop up.

"Wait," Lorne started to say.

With an heroic effort, the sparrow hopped mightily, his

one good wing beating frantically, striving to get his weight over the rim.

But he could not do it. The weight of his limp, hanging wing made the difference, and he was pulled backwards. Tumbling onto the branch with a chirp of surprise, he fluttered off, crashed heavily through the leaves, and fell to the ground below.

"Oh, no!" Lorne cried. "He fell! He fell! Spenser fell!"

"He what?" he heard Spenser's wife say. Lorne leapt from the branch and floated down as fast as his light little body could go, a flicker of orange and yellow sifting down through the leaves toward his fallen friend.

Mrs. Spenser fluttered past him and was bending over her husband when Lorne got there. He was lying unconscious beside the sticky, feathered goo and eggshells. Was he also dead?

"Spenser! My Spenser!" his wife cried, opening her wings slightly as if she would shelter his broken body from further harm.

As she spoke, Eva came walking along the path. She was holding a spray of hazelwood and was singing softly to herself. When she saw the broken bird, she dropped the branch and ran quickly to it.

"Oh, look!" she cried. "Poor sparrow. Don't worry," she said to Mrs. Spenser, who had hopped away, squawking pathetically, wondering what other dire misfortune was befalling her. "It's your mate, isn't it? I won't hurt it. Maybe I can help."

Lorne was hiding under Spenser's good wing. He knew this girl. She would probably take the injured bird home and try to nurse him back to health. That's the way she was. And if she did, Lorne intended to go along for the ride to keep an eye on his friend.

5

Lorne thought he was going to suffocate, stowed away under the sparrow's wing. He was not like a beetle or potato bug that loves to be stuffed away from the light. Far from it. But his one consolation was that he could feel his friend's heart beating and knew that he was alive. With every loud, rapid thump of that heart Lorne felt like rejoicing. Spenser was going to be all right.

Then he heard Eva call with almost deafening loudness, "Reed! Come quick! Look what I've found!"

He heard the door close, and soon they stopped moving. They were inside the humans' house.

He would have loved to have scrambled out from under the stuffy, reverberating wing, but he did not dare. He knew they did not like bugs inside the house, even ladybugs, which were popular everywhere else. He just hoped they would not get the wings mixed up and find him while they tried to heal Spenser. They would put him outside, and he would have to sneak back in, risking being crushed by a heedless heel or, worse, by the dog or cat. He had come inside once before in the girl's hair, but she did not know it. No one had seen the little orange and yellow jewel that had adorned her golden hair. He had flown to the sofa, to the desk chair, to the little table in the entranceway, and then had crawled under the door and flown away, full to bursting with tales to relate to Larry—and with pride over his daring escapade.

But now he was here for a very different reason—a much

more serious one. He would have to be a messenger between the two sparrows to keep them from worrying. He was going to have to sneak in and out a few times and stay hidden long enough to give Spenser moral support when he started to revive.

"Is it dead?" suddenly came the little boy's booming voice. "No, look, Eva! It's moving!"

"Its wing is broken," the girl said. "It must have fallen out of the tree."

"How can a bird fall out a tree?" Reed asked sensibly.

"Good question. It must have gotten hurt somehow before it fell. Ooh, I hope it lives. The poor thing. I bet it's mate is worried to death."

"Is it a boy or a girl?"

"I don't know how you tell with sparrows. With parakeets it's easy. The boys have blue over their beaks, and the girls have brown."

"It doesn't have anything over its beak except feathers," Reed said, his voice even louder as he evidently leaned for a closer look. Lorne wished he could answer some of his questions, especially the one about gender.

"What it needs right now is rest. Let's leave it alone for an hour or so and then look at it again."

"Okay. I have to meet Jay anyway."

"Is Mom home yet?" Eva asked, her voice getting farther away.

"Yes. She's upstairs writing a letter."

A door closed, and Lorne could not hear the voices anymore. It was safe to come out.

He crawled out from under the wing and saw that they were in a bird cage on the washing machine in the laundry room. At least they were safe from the animals, who were very jealous of other living creatures in the house and seemed to feel they were superior to everything that was not

a pet and had to live by its wits. They did not realize how soft and dull they had become. But they were still dangerous to ladybugs and sparrows.

Eva had put a little doll in the cage, apparently to cheer Spenser up. It looked like a cross between a monkey baby and a human baby. Lorne gave a start of fright when he first saw the doll's blue eyes looking at him as he emerged from the limp feathers. He saw it was only a doll.

When the doll spoke to him, he was even more startled. He involuntarily flew up to one of the bars and looked back with disbelieving suspicion at the furry doll. The blue eyes blinked.

"Yes, I can talk, and, yes, I'm alive," the strange creature said. "But don't worry, I prefer french fries to bugs. I won't be able to move for another generation at least. It takes a lot of love to get these limbs stirring. But how could I remain senseless—without a mind, without a heart—with dear Eva taking care of me? You'll see what I mean."

"What are you?" Lorne asked, flying back down and crawling a few inches closer to where the fuzzy brown, pink-faced, blue-eyed creature sat in a corner.

"I'm a monchichi. My name is Michiko. I come from Japan. At least my body. My life comes from Eva. She could give it to a stone. You'll see what I mean. Please come closer. I'm completely harmless." The doll spoke in a round, furry voice, an amiable and harmless voice. Lorne realized she was a reflection of Eva's personality and could be trusted. He crawled over beside the pink-bottomed foot.

"Please fly up to my knee so I can see you better."

Lorne did so and felt he was basking in some kind of warm sunlight as the two big eyes looked down at him from the shining pink face.

"Now tell me about it," Michiko said. "What happened to your friend here?"

6

As Lorne told Michiko about the crows, while being careful to say little about the nightingale at this point, the monchichi looked down at him approvingly and admiringly. The young ladybug looked very beautiful to Michiko, its orange and yellow colors glowing in the dimness like a little jewel. He reminded her of a tiny, precious bit of Japanese pottery—the way the two black bands on each orange wing were bordered by bright yellow. He looked like something that had been made with great care but with perfect, happy freedom.

Suddenly, there was a peep from the sparrow—then a chirp, then a gentle trill.

"He's coming to!" Lorne shrilled. He whirred lightly over to where his friend was stirring—the good wing stretching slightly, the eyes blinking slowly and glistening in the faded light.

Michiko realized she could understand these sounds.

"There were peacocks there," Spenser said softly, distantly, "with jewels in their tails, necks of blue gold, feathers like pine needles at dawn with a lake seen through them. There were flamingos, cool as peppermint, spreading circles of light with every careful step."

The monchichi was enchanted. "What's he talking about?" she whispered. "Do sparrows have such dreams as this?"

"It's the magic garden," Lorne said, deeply happy at

26

Spenser's awakening and at his imagery, but fearful that his brain might have been damaged.

"There were swans," Spenser sang softly. "There were swans there with their bandit masks removed and looks of childlike wonder on their dignified faces. They sailed in the sun bearing treasures of light. Over and over their majestic courses inscribed a single word upon the pond: *love*. The letters spread upon the water, blended together into rivulets of meaning until there was not a single drop in all that lustrous, liquid face that didn't tell of love."

"How beautiful!" Michiko breathed. "Is this a real place he's talking about?"

But Lorne could not answer for the moment. He was transported.

"And there was a nightingale," Spenser whispered. A limpid tear welled in his eye, reflecting for a moment Lorne's orange and yellow and black body where he stood by the beak, then sinking into Spenser's feathers.

Lorne flew to his friend's shoulder.

"Yes?" he said.

"But I have not the words to tell you of the nightingale. Obey his song."

His eyes closed. His light had flown away.

"Spenser?" Lorne said. "Spenser? I guess he's gone back to sleep."

"He's dead," Michiko said, dropping her eyes. "He's gone."

Lorne could not stop weeping for his friend for an hour or so. He stayed on Spenser's shoulder, his pinpoint tears soaking into the feathers beneath him. Gradually, he could feel the body stiffening. It wasn't Spenser any more. It was just his discarded body.

Almost as if reading his thoughts, Michiko said, "He's

gone, Lorne. That's only the form he took while he was here. He's probably a swan now, writing love letters to the nightingale on a lake of liquid jewels. Or maybe he's a kind of nightingale himself singing to a mystic rose."

"No, please don't say that," Lorne sobbed urgently. "If he really is somewhere, in some magic garden, I want him to be Spenser—to be the Spenser I loved. I want him to be brown and cream and small and honest the way he is—the way he was. He was a perfect Spenser that way."

"Maybe that's why it was time for him to go," Michiko said. "He was ready for a perfect place. This place has a lot of problems."

"Yes," Lorne said, gritting his teeth. "Crows."

"And the crows that are in each of us."

"What do you mean?"

"Remember in Spenser's song when the swans lost their black masks? They were pure white. They only loved now—it wasn't possible for them to hate or trick or get angry or anything of that sort. Their love for the nightingale made them completely pure, just as if crows lurking in their breasts had been banished."

"But I hate the crows for killing Spenser and for all of the ugly things they do every day. For keeping the nightingale a prisoner." He realized he had told the secret, but he did not regret it. The monchichi was kind and could be trusted. "Isn't it natural to feel that way?" Lorne asked.

"It may be natural, but it may not be best," Michiko answered with a round, furry voice that had an echo of Eva's speech in it. "As long as there are crows in us, the crows are winning."

As soon as Michiko said this, Lorne knew it was true. It was the message of the nightingale. When his song came pouring through the trees, there was no room left in the

28

heart for anything but love and joy and peace and happy things. Hatred was just another cawing crow.

"Yes, that's what the nightingale says," Lorne said quietly.

"He does?" Michiko's eyes grew wide and keen at the same time. She felt something tugging at her whenever the nightingale was mentioned, as if some potential for movement were beginning to stir in her.

Spenser's last words—"Obey his song"—was like a commandment for Lorne. Hearing that song, he could not help loving it. But when it had faded away, it was hard to live up to. It even seemed impossible at times. Was the monchichi right? Was it a question of chasing away crows like a farmer in a field? That must be it. Then the harvest would come.

"So the nightingale is a prisoner?" Michiko asked.

"Yes. The crows keep him on Emerald Hill. They don't let anybody in or out."

"But Spenser got in?"

"A few times—yes."

Just then the door opened, and Eva came in.

7

Eva turned on the light and almost immediately said, "Oh, what a shame! You're dead, aren't you, little bird. I'm so sorry."

Lorne huddled in a corner of the cage as the little girl bent over and gently removed Spenser's body, her long blond hair hanging for a moment like golden curtains over the cage.

"How stiff and hard you are. Dead. What does it mean? Where do we fly to, little bird?"

Quickly, Michiko whispered for Lorne to come and hide in her fur.

"Well, let's go bury him, Michiko," Eva said, reaching for the monchichi. "Everything has to die, I guess. I feel sorry for its mate."

Lorne clung to Michiko's soft, silken fur as they went into the huge living room, its plate-glass windows opening onto the lawn and the garden beyond. Dark dots—crows— filled the sky. Then for an unbelievable moment, as Eva passed through the room, Lorne thought he saw Spenser fluttering at the window. Once in the hallway, Lorne could not see any more. Was it his imagination, his wishful thinking? He was sure he had seen a sparrow there, moving in the brave and honest way of his departed friend.

When they got outside, he knew the answer. It was Spenser's wife. But she was different now. She did not shriek in anguish when she saw her mate's body, as Lorne expected she would. She seemed to know Spenser was dead.

She flew and hopped beside them as they walked, singing a poignant, mournful song. She was like a wife who has emptied herself of a week of tears and is ready for the funeral ceremony, where bereavement becomes a public thing and must be nobly borne. Lorne was impressed with her bravery. He could hardly take his eyes off her as they moved toward the grove of pine trees in the corner of the yard past the swimming pool. It was almost as if the spirit of Spenser had been resurrected in his wife.

"You're very sad, aren't you," Eva said. "I wonder why I think you're the wife and he was the husband? We'll give him a decent burial anyway, and you'll know where his body is."

The cocker spaniel came bounding up and stood on his hind legs to sniff what his mistress held. Lorne cringed at the loud snuffling of the dangerous creature.

"No you don't, Taffy! Now don't you dare tell the cat where we're burying this little sparrow, you hear me? Of course, I know you're not speaking to each other these days."

To herself she added, "I guess I really need a pick and shovel to make the hole deep enough. I wish Daddy were home. Let's see—where does he keep them?" She veered back across the yard toward the basement of the light-pink, three-storied clapboard house and hoped the cat was off hunting or doing whatever she did on her secret forays into the world.

"Reed!" she called. "Hey, Reed! We have a job to do. Where are you?"

Mrs. Spenser fluttered along, still warbling mournfully, and kept her distance from the dog. She looked lost but game, wondering what to do, but pressing on as Spenser would have done. Lorne wished he could communicate with her in some way. He knew she needed a friend's support. He also realized, with a certain shy surprise, that he needed her. Their friendship would be the best memorial to Spenser.

"Coming, Eva," came Reed's resigned reply. "Is it lunchtime already?" He emerged from the neighbor's yard through the secret passage in the honeysuckle arbor.

"The little bird died," Eva said.

Reed stopped.

"It died?" He started to say "Why?" then remembered the death of their other dog the year before. The corners of his mouth lowered as he came forward.

"Where shall we bury it?" he asked.

"In the middle of the pine trees. Let's get the pick and shovel so we can make it too deep for the cat to dig up."

Reed perked up at this.

"Okay! Wait here. I know where they are." Toward the basement he ran, leaning forward from the waist, his sturdy legs flashing in the spring sun. Soon he came back out again with the handles of the pick and shovel each clasped tightly, the metal heads clanging on the concrete walk. Reed wondered if he really could carry the two big tools but was determined to get across the yard. By the time he reached Eva, he was ready for some help.

"Would you take the shovel, Eva?"

"Okay." Eva fit Michiko into the crook of her right arm and, grasping the handle of the shovel with her left hand, dragged it behind her as she started back across the lawn. Reed held the pick before him heftily, trying not to kick it with his knees as he walked. He had to stop and rest in the middle of the yard.

"Wait for me, Eva. It's heavy!"

"Oh, look!" Eva cried. "The Ferguson's parrot!"

Strutting beside the dark grove of pine was the garish harlequin parrot that liked to imitate the nightingale. He was so brilliantly red, blue, yellow, and green that he seemed artificial, like fruits and vegetables that have been craftily treated with dye. Lorne, another creature of color, could not help feeling—perhaps somewhat out of envy— that the bright colors of the parrot contrasted with the ugliness of the look in his eye and of his lethally hooked beak. It was as if one of Joseph's meanest brothers had stolen his coat of many colors.

"Should we try to catch it?" Reed asked eagerly.

"It's impossible. And Mr. Ferguson told Daddy we shouldn't try because he bites. He's pretty, but he doesn't look very nice, really, if you look at his face."

"Have a nice day!" came a strange, thin voice.

"Who said that?" Reed asked, surprised, looking around.

"That was the parrot," Eva giggled.

"Who, me?" came the same mocking voice from beside the pines. The parrot was strutting back and forth, as if asserting his claim to belong in the human world at the same time that he reserved his right to live freely in the garden.

"Did you hear that, Eva? 'Who, me?' He talks as well as I do."

As Eva approached the circle of pines, the parrot, hopping crudely with wings half extended, disappeared with a squawk.

Lorne always had a sick feeling in his stomach when he saw the parrot, a feeling that something bad was going to happen—or already was happening. He almost believed that the parrot was one of the crows in disguise—maybe even the *king* crow. The parrot was about the same size, and his own real sound was an ugly, rough sound that was not unlike the dark, threatening caw of crows. Lorne hoped that the parrot had gone and would not see where they were going to bury Spenser. He knew that this grave would become very important to him and, of course, to Mrs. Spenser. It would be a kind of martyr's shrine where they would go to renew their faith and courage. Because of Spenser's death, it seemed they had a big job ahead of them. They had to carry on where he had left off, linking the lower garden with the higher, magical one. Lorne knew in his heart that the parrot, who loved his own imitation more than the nightingale's song, would be an enemy in this venture.

8

It was Reed's turn to dig. Holding the pick with both hands down toward the head, the handle between his legs, he wedged up a few more clods with the pointed side.

They were among the pines in a kind of dark little room carpeted with a springy orange-brown layer of pine needles. Spenser lay inert under one of the trees, his head limp. Michiko sat beside him and watched wonderingly with her blue eyes in her pink face. Lorne gazed at Eva and Reed while Reed bent over in earnest effort.

Eva stood by holding the shovel and waiting for her next turn.

Mrs. Spenser hopped anxiously in the light at the doorway of the grove, looking back and forth between the dog watching on the far side of the room and the sweet, still body of her dead husband.

"Here, let me scoop it out now," Eva said. Reed straightened up with some relief and dropped the pick beside the hole as if it were suddenly very hot.

"Whew!" he said. "I think it's deep enough now. We'll get to China soon!"

Eva moved over, pressed the blade of the shovel carefully into the five-inch hole, and drew out a spilling mound of dirt. Finally, after a few of these maneuvers, the hole seemed ready.

"That should do it." Eva laid the shovel down beside the pick and tenderly picked the sparrow up, careful to cradle the dangling head.

"Can you see, Mrs. Sparrow?" she asked over her shoulder toward the sunlight.

Then she drew her breath in and turned around quickly toward the opening. She saw a strange sight, one that reminded her of what they had learned about food chains in science class.

The sparrow was hopping back and forth in the opening. Just behind her was the big, garish parrot, bright and fearsome as an open wound, looking as if he were ready to attack the smaller bird. And just beyond him was the crouching, creeping cat, stealing up on this incredible prey.

For a moment, seeing that hooked face, Eva was tempted to let Mildred catch the parrot. But her kindly heart got the better of her just as the cat gathered up her muscles for a prehistoric leap.

"Don't you dare, Mildred!" she shouted, rushing for the opening in the pines. The sparrow fluttered away, the parrot gave a squawk and a heavy little backward hop, and the cat shot like a low missile into the far edge of the pines, the energy of attack converted into the energy of escape.

The parrot blurted some unintelligible human syllables, collected itself, and flew away toward the garden as it trailed squawks like curses.

"At least you could thank me instead of swearing at me," Eva said, watching the parrot go with a strange feeling of foreboding.

"What happened?" Reed asked.

"Oh, Mildred was about to attack the parrot. And I'm not sure, but I think the parrot was about to attack the sparrow."

Reed giggled at the way Eva said this.

Just as they turned back to the little burial ceremony, the sun reached its meridian. In a matter of seconds the tiny clearing was flooded with light.

"Look!" Eva cried. "The sun! It must be time to bury him."

"Here's the mother sparrow," Reed said. Mrs. Spenser was hopping in the pathway again. She began a soft, gentle trilling, a song not so much of death, it seemed, as of quiet hearth and home.

"Oh, good!"

Lorne, in the meantime, could contain himself no longer. He crawled out of the silky fur, and, leaping lightly out onto the air, sailed over to the edge of the grave, where he fairly sparkled in the light against the moist, dark earth.

"Eva! Another ladybug! See? Right beside you. It's the same kind as the last time."

"How pretty it is!" Eva exclaimed, pausing for a moment to gaze down at the orange and yellow gleaming bead. "It looks so bright and fresh, doesn't it?"

"Maybe it's the sparrow's friend," Reed said earnestly.

Eva laughed, looking more carefully at the bug. "Maybe so. Anyway, it makes it all seem more cheerful."

Bending forward with the limp body in both hands, she said, as if to the insect, "Watch carefully now. You won't see your friend again."

Lorne winced at this—and was not convinced. He thought of the nightingale. What would his opinion be?

Eva quickly stooped down and laid Spenser in the shadowed grave. The orange pine needles seemed almost to burn with a soft fire in the sunlight. After a moment Eva spoke again.

"Let's say a prayer, even though he is just a bird."

The two children stood on either side of the grave, hands before them, heads bowed like offerings of gold to the sun that gleamed in their hair. Eva recited a short prayer their father had taught them:

"'Say: God sufficeth all things above all things, and

nothing in the heavens or in the earth but God sufficeth. Verily, He is in Himself the Knower, the Sustainer, the Omnipotent.'"

With a brisk motion Eva picked up the shovel and poured dirt on the body. Reed squatted down and started shoving the little piles back into place. Soon Spenser's body was hidden from sight by a thick veil of earth.

When the last clods of dirt had been spilled onto the body and packed into place, the children scattered pine needles over it to hide it from digging animals. Watching intently, Lorne suddenly felt an eager, new resolve to carry on where Spenser had left off. He glanced at Mrs. Spenser, who stood still in the pathway and seemed oblivious of the dog, and he sensed that she was feeling the same renewed spirit of following in her husband's pathway. He was again amazed at her new demeanor and also felt that sense of resurrection.

He rose softly off the earth, shrilled a good-bye to Michiko, and flashed through the sunlight to Mrs. Spenser, who, with a sudden rush of hopefulness, saw him coming.

"There goes the ladybug!" Reed cried.

"Watch this!" Lorne thought. He landed lightly on Mrs. Spenser's shoulder, burrowed down at the base of her neck, and, as at a secret signal, they were off.

Eva dropped the handful of pine needles she still held.

"Wow! Did you see that!" Reed cried.

Eva was speechless for a moment, then said softly, "That was amazing!"

Reed rushed to the opening in the trees and peered up.

"I wish *I* could do that," he said.

Eva walked up beside him, and the two children—sister and brother—stood in the sunlit pathway in the pines looking out wonderingly at the sky.

38

9

Night. What was a crow and what merely a corner of the darkness? Where were the guards posted along the base of the hill? A sense of movement in the inky blackness off to their left froze them still. Both had sensed it, and both craned with barely controlled terror in that vague, threatening direction. Lorne peeked out from Mrs. Spenser's neck feathers. He had learned to feel safe and snug there, but in the dark danger of this night, he felt his sense of security diminishing fast. How could they get past this black wall and into the garden of light?

Then there was a movement in front of them—a branch stirring in a slight breeze. The first must have been a false alarm, too. The tiny sparrow at the foot of the big hill took another hop into the huge mouth of night.

The northwest angle was the best, according to what Mrs. Spenser could remember her husband's saying. Why had she not listened more seriously? But she realized she had heard more than she would have admitted at the time. Spenser's enthusiasm was contagious, and she had acted disinterested and condescending. Why? For balance, to keep things in order? But something in her had always responded, like a compass needle. How could she have resisted? They were one thing, really. Now half of that was gone. Spenser was dead. Death was like this black wall of night— but Mrs. Spenser could not help feeling that there was light on the other side, higher up. And she could not help feeling that brave, wise, lovable Spenser was with them.

And her babies?

She could not face that mystery yet.

She was hopping into this dragon's den in a sense for them—for the future they might have had. What might she and Lorne learn from the nightingale?

"Nightingale! Nightingale!" she whispered softly.

At last they heard the fluid, poignant song. Did he know they were coming and needed this reassurance? His voice shattered the blackness into a mosaic of inner-lit colors, like a stained-glass window in a church. The swelling, trilling, heart-rending, heart-warming music flowed upon them in soothing waves. Robes of comfort seemed to wrap softly around them. "Yes, come," the birdsong seemed to say. "Press on. We are waiting."

And the crows? Would they give their positions away by clamoring to drown out the healing song? Lorne and Mrs. Spenser waited in suspense, listening, as the last notes faded down the hillside to sweeten many dreams.

The beautiful sound reminded Mrs. Spenser of the night, soon after Spenser's death, when she had been awakened by a soft, lovely song coming from a nearby tree. She knew it was the nightingale and that he was singing just for her. She knew then that he was not really a prisoner but that she somehow was. He told her to escape the lower garden: she must get past the crows. In the morning it had seemed like a dream, but in her heart she knew the song was real.

The silence deepened once again, punctuated by far-off rustlings and the whirr and chirr of insects Mrs. Spenser could not name. She only went out during the daytime and did not know the goings on of night. She hopped, and hopped, and hopped, and gradually they made their way up through the undergrowth at the foot of the hill.

It was a humbling experience—Mrs. Spenser realized with a sigh—as well as a terrifying one. It stung her pride to have to advance by slow degrees along the ground with her perfectly flyable wings tucked neatly at her sides. But she dared not approach by air—not with the hawk guards Spenser told of with awe, that cadre of well-trained dive-bombers that could shoot higher and drop faster than anything on wings. They were brainwashed machines of the dark crows' bidding and took pride in eliminating any bird that entered the airways above Emerald Hill. Yes, Mrs. Spenser was forced to hop, hop, hop up the hill like a feathery little toad and hoped she could sneak by the raven sentinel.

A small, shrill whisper pierced her ear.

"Mrs. Spenser!" Lorne called from the back of her neck. "By the big elm! By the big elm! Remember?"

"Yes, Lorne, that's right. It comes back to me now. Spenser mentioned that to me as well."

"The guard gets sleepy there," Lorne whispered excitedly.

"Yes." Mrs. Spenser could not restrain a small, inward chuckle touched with irony. To herself she murmured, "His nest is in that tree, and his mate, and he feels too much at home to do his dastardly job." To Lorne she whispered, "Yes, Lorne. The big elm." And indeed, she recalled, it was on the northwest side.

What an adjustment it took, she sighed, to get into this adventure business. She was made for nests and the cozy warmth of fledging feathers . . . Ah well, there was a real need all right, a very practical need. She would be a different kind of mother. Something had to be done about crows that ravaged homes. And about the nightingale, who seemed to have so much to tell them.

But the darkness seemed to close around them, and her thoughts were broken off. Wings of night, jagged and black, swooped upon them from all sides. A huge black claw clamped her to the sodden earth. They were caught.

She felt limp with terror and despair. "Hide, Lorne!" came the thought. He burrowed down toward the base of her wings away from the iron pressure of the claw. It hurt her, that claw, and she chirped in pain.

"What have we here?" came a gruff, gravelly voice.

"I think it's Spenser's wife, Sergeant," said another.

"Looking for your little hubbie, are you?" rasped the first voice, the voice of the crow that held her. "Would you like to follow him, snug little Mrs. Spenser? We'll be happy to dispatch you."

From where her head was laid out flat on a fallen leaf, the sparrow looked up at the nightmare of her captors.

Three curving swords seemed to be aimed at her from high in the night sky, and six malevolent stars seemed to be beaming a hideous light of malice upon her. The darkness shuddered and shook with the strong, clumsy movements of the three self-congratulating crows.

"The boss'll be pleased at this, Sergeant Thorndrug," came the second voice, hollow and ugly but with a slight whine in it of anxiety to please.

"Over a sparrow?" scoffed the first like a bear trap, his beak clacking shut with emphasis and his claw convulsing so noisily that Mrs. Spenser cried out unheard. "He's not interested in no sparrow. It's the doves he wants, man! Ain't you learned that yet? Raise your sights! It's doves we're after. Sparrows are all in a night's work."

Daring to look up again, Mrs. Spenser could see them better now, their hulking, angular forms.

The third crow, a female, spoke now:

"I wouldn't look down your beak at the elimination of Spenser, if I were you, Thorndrug. The boss was pleased. I suspect you're a bit envious since you had no part in that caper."

"Well, so . . ." the first muttered grudgingly. "I got his

mate, and you darn better make sure the boss gets it straight. *I* saw her, and *I* got her, and *I* had better get the credit!"

With every utterance of the word *I* the first crow gripped with his claw in such a way that Mrs. Spenser thought she would always hate that word forever after. But would there be an ever after?

"Maybe we'd better question her to see how much Spenser told her," the second one said rather quickly, as if he were not too sure of himself.

"Idiot!" the first one scoffed.

But before he could continue, he heard a sound of assent from the third and realized it was a good idea.

"Of course, we should, fool! Why say it?" he continued.

"I suggest we take her to the boss," the third one said with a pondering air. There was a sound of conspiracy in her voice.

Mrs. Spenser felt helpless. How could she possibly get out of this? Would she not reach the nightingale after all? But would she reach Spenser?

"Stay hidden, Lorne," she thought. "It will be a long way for you by yourself on those tiny wings, but perhaps you can get through. Look for your chance to slide off my back and sneak away. You are our only hope."

It did not occur to Mrs. Spenser that it would not occur to Lorne to abandon her. He flattened down as far as he could under the terrible, taloned pressure. He must see where they were taking her and then hope that a good idea would come. He wished the nightingale would sing again to give them hope.

"Who knows what seeds of interest that sparrow may have planted that might begin to sprout," the third one croaked from a little farther away. "It's best we nip them in the bud."

"Hey, I get it!" the second exclaimed. "Seeds, sprouts, buds. Very clever, Sergeant Franklemummer!"

"Get what?" Thorndrug mumbled, having missed the analogy. "The strategy seems pretty obvious to me. Let's get flapping." The captor crow wrenched her off the ground, his strong talons curving around the sides of her body and clamping her so tightly that she could hardly breathe. Then, with violent hops that all but smashed her, and in a loose, sinister commotion of big, black wings, the crow ponderously gained a berth on the air and carried Mrs. Spenser and Lorne toward the leader of all these cruel and ugly creatures.

10

Flying up into a large, dead tree with four or five crow's nests hanging overhead like monstrous bats, they came to a hole in the trunk that was the entrance to the boss' chambers. Entering the dark hollow, lit dimly by a quarter moon that had scythed its way through the cloud cover, Mrs. Spenser had a momentary sense of hope at the sudden glimpse of a garden of colors in the gloom. When she saw who owned the colors, however, her sense of despair grew deeper than before—and a new chill of terror tingled down her spine.

Should she have been surprised?

The "boss" was the Fergusons' parrot, the one who dared to mimic the nightingale's song.

"Blast it!" the parrot squawked. "Drat you satans anyway! I was just dropping off."

"We are very sorry to disturb you, sire," Franklemummer said politely. "But you said . . ."

"I know, I know, I know, I *know!* Come in! Come in! What is it this time? *Stop hanging back like a bunch of timid doves!*" He shouted these last words so loudly that his voice echoed up and down the length of the hollow tree. The parrot was obviously in a foul mood.

"Dreams, dreams," he muttered as they entered. "Can't get away from them. *Not fair,* blast it!"

Mrs. Spenser trembled for a moment in a spasm of fear. She felt so utterly helpless in the midst of these huge, strong-beaked birds, which seemed to hate her so much for reasons she could not fathom. What had she and Spenser ever done to them? What was so bad about trying to talk to a bird with a beautiful song?

And then the night-song came again, the day-song sung at night. The clear, penetrating notes—so limpid and yet so full—seemed aimed right at the parrot's hollow. They came pouring in like a flock of invisible, invincible birds flying confidently to a rescue.

For a moment the parrot turned away and groaned, hunching the shoulders of his bright wings and lowering his big, hook-beaked head as if to bury it in the red, yellow, blue, and green feathers.

"Go! Go! Sing! Sing!" he squawked suddenly over his shoulder. Then, as the three crows bumped into each other, jostling and ruffling to get out of the hole, he yelled, "No, drat it! Stay here. What's the use. Save your lungs for tomorrow."

He stood with his back turned and his head lowered for a moment as the last notes resounded gaily along the inside of the dead tree.

"No one's listening anyway," he said in a quieter voice. "I try those higher and lower notes over and over again," he lamented despairingly as if to himself. "I don't know how he does it. Don't breathe a word of this, officers. You are privy tonight; you are privy. Some of his effects are simply beyond me."

The words startled Mrs. Spenser, not for the confession of failure they expressed but for the total lack of self-knowledge they evinced. It astonished her that he should imagine that any one of his notes resembled the nightingale's in the slightest way. Oh yes, he may have repeated the same melody. But the song, the true inner music, was absolutely different: One was beautifully real, the other an ugly imitation. Was he trying to compete with the nightingale?

A new dimension was added to her fear at the realization of the lunacy that had engulfed her.

"Why did you come this evening, officers?" the parrot asked, controlling himself. Mrs. Spenser was now aware that these words, too, were an imitation and that the "boss" of all the ruthless crows was as hollow as his tree.

Thorndrug lurched forward, eagerly holding out the claw that was full of Mrs. Spenser.

"I—we got Spenser's mate, your Majesty," he announced obsequiously.

Glancing at the claw full of brown feathers, the leader replied, "And who, pray tell, is Spenser? Another sparrow, I take it."

Thorndrug glanced at the other crows as if to say, "See what I mean? The boss and I understand these things."

"The one . . . ," Franklemummer began.

Franklemummer's voice seemed to bring the memory back to the parrot, as if he were losing touch with his affairs and relying heavily on the intelligence of crows like Franklemummer.

"Yes, I know, I know. The little mosquito that had to be swatted."

The hooked beak, glaring eyes, and blaring hues suddenly leaned down on limp Mrs. Spenser as if in attack. She recoiled in terror in the tightening grip.

"Looking for your nice little mate, are you, Mrs. Morsel? I bet you're proud of him and imagine he died for a beautiful cause. What a joke! We give him a stern warning, and he faints for fear and falls out of his own tree."

The tree trunk clamored for a minute from the false, raucous laughter of the three crows showing how witty they thought their leader was.

Mrs. Spenser chirped a few words of truth in self-forgetful defense of her husband, but a quick, powerful squeeze

48

took her breath away and made her reel for a moment on the edge of consciousness.

"We don't like your kind coming up the hillside, Mrs. Morsel," the parrot went on, warming up and seeming to find a new lease on life. "It's you humble types that often cause the most trouble, getting the sympathy of the humans and always acting so harmless that you're hardly noticed. How I loathe those chirps of yours, those quick hops on the lawn, that way you have of jerking your head around in all directions. It makes my heartily sick. You've hopped about one hop too many, Spenser's wife!"

Suddenly, a sense of joy and release welled in the sparrow's little breast, and she welcomed the thought of the blows that seemed about to fall. "I'm coming, Spenser!"

11

What was he to do?

Lorne had wormed his way around to the deep, soft breast feathers, where he huddled like the hidden, gem-like soul of the hapless bird. He was away from the pressure points of all of the talons for now. But what good could he do here? What good could he do anywhere, for that matter? Could he get to the top of the hill himself? How could they possibly see him at night, even with their searchlight vision? Perhaps he should have come alone in the first place and not drawn Mrs. Spenser into such disaster. But she had insisted on coming.

It seemed that he could only choose his course by a process of elimination. Staying here would serve no purpose. He could never defend her against four lethal beaks and eight trap-like claws, and he could see no way to help her escape. He had to get to the nightingale. Though the songbird was a prisoner, it seemed the only way.

His own escape did not seem difficult. As the croakings and squawkings continued above him like jagged panes of glass being hurled across the room, he tunneled his way down the sparrow's breast to her stomach, signaling to her, he hoped, the move he was making. At a point near where a talon was locked against the soft underbelly, Lorne peeked out. His first image was of the quarter moon and moving clouds, seen through the hole in the hollow trunk—his escape route. His second was of the wild eyes and hooked beak of the parrot, perched on a shelf-like knot above them, and pontificating to his sheepish but treacherous-looking crows. Even in the gloom, the parrot was a sunburst of colors. For a moment, Lorne was ashamed of his own bright coloration, another gay livery signifying nothing.

Quickly, he crawled down to a rotting knot, slipped along a shadowed groove to the inner wall of the trunk, sped up it like a colorful raindrop sliding up a windshield, and reached the threshold of the parrot's domain. Just as he was about to launch himself into the grinning night, the parrot squawked with outraged alarm:

"What the devil! Who's that? Stop him, officers! Get him!"

As Franklemummer hopped and then lunged with a clack of her beak, Lorne opened his tiny wings and whirred from the threshold out into the night. He spiraled down around the trunk half a turn as he listened to the hurried flapping above him and, alighting, deftly slid under an edge of bark and waited.

A shadowy wing dropped past, the long feather-fingers seeming to brush like claws against the very lid of his hiding place. Then the shadow swept by again, this time going up. Lorne cowered from a knife of light hurled by the dagger moon. His orange and yellow must not be seen. A third time, a fourth—the powerful wings stroked by in their almost delicate, tip-lifted way. He heard a commotion of arrival above and a subdued croaking from inside the tree and knew he was safe—at least for now.

They no doubt had given up on him as being insignificant. And how insignificant he felt. Peeking out of the little corner of bark, he was astonished at the size of the hillside forest. For him to ascend alone was like a single man climbing Mount Everest. An endless crowd of giant trees loomed in the thin light. Did he have the strength—or even the time—to make it to the top? And if he did attain the presence of the nightingale through the ministrations of a kindly fate, what could a prisoner do to help another prisoner in another jail escape? And would Mrs. Spenser be dead by then? His path, indeed, seemed merely the lesser of two evils, and a sense of despondency paralyzed him for a moment where he clung to the dead tree.

The dead tree! His whole body seemed to shrink with repulsion. "Get going," he said to himself, "and get away from this hateful, death-dealing place, and aim for the top!"

Out the orange, black, and yellow drop poured, like a drop of paint, and then sailed lightly out into the air. He drifted down, down, down, invisible to any but an eye that already knew he was there, landed near a pile of parrot droppings, pulled back with disgust, and started on his steadfast journey.

12

In what resembled long, slow-motion hops Lorne gradually advanced up the wooded side of Emerald Hill. From leaf, to twig, to needle, to log, to stone, to stream—no, fly over the stream!—to wet stone, to grass blade, to . . . (rest, bug, rest!), Lorne nibbled at the monstrous night. Every shadowed corner around him wierdly assumed the shape of a crow. Looking up from the vantage point of a boulder, he was dismayed to find that the distance seemed about the same as when he had started. But perhaps it was an illusion of the darkness. Surely he had made significant progress.

It was then that he heard the muffled croaking of another crow.

Though the voice was low, its owner was startlingly near. Lorne sped into a tiny cave in the boulder and craned to hear. A second voice came but not a crow's—a higher, clearer, sharper sound, though also held to a level just above a whisper. It was another bird, but of a species Lorne was not familiar with. The voice, though muted, had a ring of authority.

The voices were getting nearer. The two birds were slowly walking his way, deep in conversation. Lorne backed into the cave as far as he could go. Then a slimy voice behind him spoke.

"An early breakfast on a silver platter, is it?"

A long, thin tongue flickered out from around the corner of what had seemed the rear of the cave.

A lizard!

Lorne froze with sudden fear.

With a slithering flash, the lizard whipped past him, blocked the entrance, and looked back with two gigantic black eyes attached to his rubbery head.

"Aren't you a colorful little guy!" insinuated the reptile, his voice seeming to flick out like his hungry tongue.

"How kind of you to serve up my predawn repast. Will you come home to my mouth without a fuss, or are we to have a little sport?"

Lorne finally found his voice.

"I really doubt that you would like my taste, Mr. Lizard. I've seen people get sick on us before."

"I've had your kind, little guy—though I appreciate the gustatorial warning. The shell I won't touch, admittedly. But the bit of flesh I regard as a delicacy. Housefly with class, you might say. Or housefly under glass."

The whole rubbery, almost transparent, length of the lizard shivered and vibrated with mute, wicked mirth over the rhymed conceit. The lifting, lashing tail was alarmingly close to Lorne.

"Come, pretty bug, come!"

The long tail began to draw away as the long snout and flicking tongue slowly approached, hanging ominously in the air like a cobra's head.

In a flash the lizard charged, and, just as quickly, Lorne rose off the ground and sailed up to a ledge beneath the roof. The lizard froze as he landed, poised on a pinpoint, utterly immobile and yet the very embodiment of latent action. Suddenly, with his suction feet, he darted up the wall. Lorne launched again and, staying clear of the stone, flew toward the entrance of the cave. Shooting along the wall, the lizard arrived just as he did and leaped after him. But he buzzed out the opening to freedom.

And almost flew straight into the beak of a large crow!

"What's this?" the crow exclaimed, mildly startled.

Lorne tried to dodge around the black-beaked face, but almost instinctively, the crow reached up and snapped him out of the air.

Caught! Was this the end?

13

Mrs. Spenser lay tied up in the corner of a knot in the hollow tree. Ants charged eagerly around her in all directions, preparing for a feast. She could hear the tiny, electric buzzing of their excited conversation, but she could not catch any words. She had reached a peaceful state of utter resignation and complete renunciation of any attachment to life. It was not a despairing, numbed condition but a tingling, blissful one of keenest anticipation. She felt with certainty that she would soon be joining her beloved husband in some higher garden where a nightingale poured out his blissful melodies. She gazed down at the busy insects with fond, shining eyes. "Soon, little ones, soon," she even whispered.

Thorndrug loomed over her again and hauled her up with his careless claw.

"Take her to your place for now, Sergeant Thorndrug," the parrot said in his jagged, puffed-up voice. "Maybe the ants will start to jog her memory a bit more, and we can get a better list of who Spenser talked to. Especially the doves. I'm particularly interested in the doves."

"Right, boss!" Thorndrug croaked smugly. He would show that Franklemummer woman a thing or two. There were other ways besides ants to get information . . .

14

Lorne was unhurt but helpless in the clamp of the young crow's beak. Staring out with terror, he saw that the crow's companion was a fierce-looking hawk. He had never been so close to a hawk before—and would have chosen to be deprived of the experience. "But you only die once," he thought with despair.

"Whatchu got?" the hawk asked with mild curiosity, breaking off their quiet, intense conversation to glance with keen eyes at the orange, yellow, and black bubble in his companion's mouth.

" '*Ay* bug," the crow managed to say over his mouthful.

"Eat them?" the hawk asked, already obviously losing interest and looking sharply around at the dark forest with a certain distrust.

The crow shook his head. With a rather gentle jerk, he tossed Lorne into the air and watched the colorful bug disappear into the darkness.

"Ladybug, ladybug, fly away home," he called softly. Slightly embarrassed, he glanced at the hawk and explained, "That's what the human children always say."

Lorne, flying free, was astonished, *delirious* at his good fortune—but even more so at the unusual natures of these two birds. They were so different from other birds of prey. At a safe distance in the darkness, he lighted on a twig and strained to hear them, overwhelmingly curious.

"What about Franklemummer?" he heard the hawk ask.

They seemed to have stopped walking for the moment and were lingering beside the boulder.

"No—not yet, anyway," the crow replied with soft croakings. "He doesn't worship the parrot anymore, but he still worships himself."

"Yes, that's the biggest hurdle, isn't it," the hawk said with a note of disgust.

"I would count nineteen or twenty of us at this point out of the flock of seventy-three. It's just a matter of time, Havenson. We're all coming around to the nightingale's side."

Lorne couldn't believe what he heard. Insurrection, subversion, revolution! Or rather: awakening, cleansing, salvation. The crows had hearts after all—and were being changed.

"And how many among you fellows?" the crow was asking.

"If I give the word, our cadre of twelve, to a bird, would turn against the parrot and his henchmen. They obey me to the letter by now."

"Does the nightingale know all this?"

"You'd better believe he knows!" the hawk replied exultantly and in a tone of fierce devotion. "He wants to win them over peacefully—that is, he wants *truly* to win them over. But I think he would like the process speeded up so he can reach the doves and sparrows and other less . . . violent and assertive creatures down there. What is your opinion, Cransome? . . . But what's this?"

Lorne had landed on the boulder at their eye level and was whirring his wings and shouting to get their attention.

15

"Mr. Cravenson! Mr. Handsome! Mr. Cravenson! Mr. Handsome! Please! Please! Listen to me!" Lorne cried.

The crow and the hawk stared at the ladybug with amused wonderment.

"Now which is which, little friend?" the crow asked. "It makes a difference with names like that."

Lorne was too excited with his discovery to pay any attention to the crow's gentle irony.

"They caught a sparrow, and they're going to kill her!" he cried.

"I'm afraid that's not so unusual," the hawk said with a certain weariness. "Where did this happen?"

"They're in the parrot's tree now!" Lorne was so beside himself he was doing little slow-motion hops on the boulder, his tiny wings whirring like a hummingbird's. "It's Spenser's wife!"

The hawk and the crow looked at each other.

"Stout-hearted little Spenser," the hawk said.

"The nightingale praised him," the crow recalled. Looking quickly back at Lorne, he softened his tone:

"Fly up here, little friend. You may as well come along. Who knows—you may come in handy!" Bending his head, he offered his strong ebony shoulders as the ladybug's perch. Against that satiny black, the orange and yellow and black bead looked more regal than ever, even in the wan moonlight.

"You'll find that with a little burrowing you can get

down under the surface, hard as it seems. We'll both be safer that way," Cransome said. Turning to Havenson then, he spoke gravely:

"You realize we may be—pardon the expression—opening a can of worms?"

"Yes," the hawk replied grimly. "Perhaps the time has come for us to stand up and be counted. I feel pretty badly about what happened to little Spenser."

"Well, let's try to talk our way through it, and, if that doesn't work . . . we'll just see what happens."

"Right."

With that the hawk and the crow hopped to the boulder and flung themselves into the air, their strong wings flapping.

What a flight it was for Lorne. He seemed to be riding all of nature as he knew it. All of the power and grace of things around him seemed to have sprouted wings and, suddenly, with a determined, regular rocking motion, borne him aloft toward a realm of heroic action. Daring to peek out, he saw Havenson the hawk soar effortlessly beside them through the trees, his scalloped wings seeming almost to touch the crow's finger-like ones. There was a look of grim urgency and resolve on his strong, fearsome face.

"Stay down!" Cransome commanded over his shoulder as they swooped into the dead tree and alighted on a gnarled, flimsy branch above the level of the entrance.

They heard no voices at first from the parrot's chambers. Above them, three black heads protruded over the rims of three nests.

"Cransome? That you?" a steely voice demanded.

"Right, Dirks," Cransome replied, echoing the tone. "Go back to bed. I won't bother the boss if he isn't awake. It can wait until morning."

"Right, right," the guard said and disappeared.

Then they heard a voice from within the hollow tree. It was unmistakably the parrot's voice, but it conveyed an uncharacteristic tone of vague bewilderment. They realized he was talking in his sleep. Moving closer to the trunk and leaning forward slightly, they listened.

"Sure, make it hurt, Thorndrug, you phoney! Givittu her good! She's a nothing, a nobody. Is that right? Nightingale . . . he said something. A nothing sparrow. Couldn't hurt a fly. What was that? *Wouldn't* hurt a fly. Brave little bugger, that Spenser. Special song for him. *I couldn't sing it! I couldn't sing it!* Who does he think he is? Just because he happens to sing so good. Who is he? . . . Who am I? My feathers are the most beautiful. A king of the trees, my mommy used to say. Strut, strut, puff, puff! Playing soldiers and the king with little Petey Parakeet. You didn't have to die that day, did you, Petey-boy? I was only playing. Lying there with your . . . bright feathers, and Mrs. Smith-Kenrick came in and took you away. The Fergusons give bigger helpings. Hello, hello! Polly wanna Sugar Smack! Have a good day, you turkey! Kids taught me some bad words."

Over his shoulder the hawk shot a keen glance, conveying a mixture of amusement, disgust, and new understanding. The crow nodded and craned forward slightly to indicate he thought it important that they listen a little longer. Lorne, astonished, could hardly restrain the gigglings that vibrated his little frame.

"*I* have lived with humans!" the parrot's voice declared with thespian emphasis. "*I* have eaten their leftovers. *I* have wandered into the bathroom while the kids were splashing in the tub. *I* have watched the missus sitting before the mirror all morning putting on makeup and drying her tears. *I* have leaped cleverly out of the way when the mister came home drunk and nearly fell on me. *I* have heard the nightingale sing. I mean . . . One night I heard it through the window, and I thought now *that's* a *performance!* Do that kind of thing instead of this see-you-later-alligator Polly-wanna-piece-of-carrot-cake business. That's a king's song! But you're a *nothing, turkey* . . ."

The last statement dropped from puffed-up theatrics to a startlingly naked tone of bitter truth in a voice the waking parrot might have used to upbraid cruelly or condemn one of his inferiors.

The rest were fragments—a few squawks, bits and snatches of nightingale imitation, human slogans and swearwords, shouted commands, then childish weeping, then sputterings, and then silence from within the dead, hollow tree.

16

Cransome and Havenson knew they must act quickly. Perhaps they had listened for too long. Thorndrug might be torturing her.

They found Thorndrug and Mrs. Spenser at the base of Thorndrug's tree on a flat space of dirt. A small bonfire was burning beside them, and it lit up the scene ghoulishly.

Thorndrug at first seemed to be peering intently into the open top of a wine jug. Then they saw the bound sparrow dangling from Thorndrug's beak by a string tied around her legs. He was lowering her slowly into a bottle. A scorpion at the bottom of the bottle arched his poisonous stinger high over his back. Mrs. Spenser's wide-eyed face was but an inch or so above the lethal, ready weapon.

"Sergeant Thorndrug!" Cransome croaked commandingly as they flew into the light and flapped to a landing.

Thorndrug started, a little like a boy caught at the cookie jar. Then he looked up with annoyance and disappointment etched on his coarse, cruel face.

"Order from the boss, Sergeant! Take her out! She's to be flown down the base of the hill and released as an object lesson for others. Take her out, I say!"

Reluctantly, mumbling something unintelligible in a frustrated tone, Thorndrug raised his head and drew out the limp, dangling sparrow with the kind, shining eyes. He dumped her on the ground, looked wryly at the two birds, and was suddenly frightened by the fact that a hawk was sent as well.

"Now what's this?" he inquired, trying to collect his dignity, but his voice shaking slightly nevertheless.

"Untie her legs!" Cransome ordered, not answering the question. "She is to be healthy enough to make it home. She will inform the others of the dangers involved in coming up the hill."

"Yes, Lieutenant, I understand," Thorndrug replied obsequiously. "She'll have something to say all right," he said with perverse glee.

Across Cransome's face flashed a look of pain, which he converted to an expression of increased sternness.

"You may now get rid of the scorpion," he ordered. "As you know, they are a danger to the young ones and should be destroyed when encountered. You will tip the bottle over and destroy the scorpion—after you have untied the sparrow's legs."

"Yeh-yes, sir!" Thorndrug replied, pulling at the string that bound Mrs. Spenser's feet.

Mrs. Spenser's head was spinning from the sickening fumes of the wine jug and from the horrible danger she had just escaped. Her legs were free now. Two crows and a hawk loomed above her. She must get away. Through the fog of dizziness and terror the thought of flight beaconed to her.

Fluttering weakly, falling and getting up again, the game sparrow hopped toward the edge of the light.

"Mrs. Spenser! Wait!" Cransome called out. With a series of stroking hops he came between her and the dark and stood above her.

She looked up at him sideways with one bright, curious eye. "Who are you?" she asked.

"Lieutenant Cransome, ma'am. We're friends."

The fog of panic seemed to have cleared in Mrs. Spenser's mind. Breathing heavily but with relief, she whispered, "The nightingale . . . Do you love his song?"

"Yes, I do."

"And does the hawk?"

"Yes, he certainly does," Cransome replied quickly, but in a low voice to keep Thorndrug from hearing. "And after we finish one important bit of business, we'll take you to meet the nightingale."

"Thank you, Lieutenant," Mrs. Spenser murmured. "I would like that." But she wondered where Lorne was.

Cransome turned back to Thorndrug, more zealous than ever to see that justice should be done. "Okay, Sergeant," he said in an official voice, "tip it over." Havenson stood back at the edge of the light and eyed Thorndrug sharply.

The bottle clattered hollowly over at the bird's nudging, and the scorpion crawled slowly out, tail raised, ready for anything.

"Nice of you fellows to let me go," came his daggerlike voice, attempting unsuccessfully to sound amiable, a role he could not abide and could only play halfheartedly even under these circumstances.

"I think I'll just walk over here to this roof of rock and crawl harmlessly away," he said.

"Think again," the hawk said.

"We don't like your poisonous kind," Cransome commented. "Go ahead, Sergeant Thorndrug. He's all yours. Give him one for the regiment. You're a pretty tough guy, aren't you?"

"Uh, sure, Lieutenant," Thorndrug said somewhat dubiously, watching the raised stinger. Not wanting to have to deal with the creature, he had forced his wife to trap the insect in the first place. Several fledglings had died from scorpion stings.

"They are nasty little buggers," he said in agreement. "Fierce . . . little buggers, even." He took a step toward the insect and lowered his beak.

"I'll just quietly crawl on home and leave you fellows to your important business," said the scorpion, but with a new note of impending danger in his voice.

"Go ahead, Sergeant," the hawk said with mild contempt. "Show us what you can do."

Then Mrs. Spenser chirped from her place on the ground. The blazing fire threw confused shadows against the tree and the ground beyond.

"Why don't you let him go, friends? He was trapped into it and is not really responsible."

"This is general policy, Mrs. Spenser," Cransome replied quickly. "It has nothing necessarily to do with your situation. Go ahead, Thorndrug."

"Gentlemen!" Mrs. Spenser said more forcefully. "I think you should let the scorpion go."

There was a long moment of silence during which all the creatures in the fitfully lit clearing stared at the sparrow. A note of authority in her voice drew their attention.

She spoke again, in a tone that seemed almost disembodied, that seemed to come from above them. "Let's try it *another* way for once, shall we?"

Cransome and Havenson looked at each other, then at Thorndrug, then at the scorpion. They both smiled at the comedy of their perplexed unison.

"Okay, brother scorpion, back to the rocks," Cransome finally said.

Slipping away, his tail arched over his head, the scorpion stopped at the threshold of the darkness. He seemed hardly able to pull himself away. "I thank you," he said at last, and was gone.

"Sergeant, go to bed," Cransome ordered with a hint of disgust.

"Yes, sir. If you will excuse me, sir," Thorndrug stammered. Hastily he withdrew into the shadows and flapped off into the night.

From beneath Cransome's jet-black feathers Lorne crawled into the scope of the firelight.

"Lorne!" Mrs. Spenser cried.

They were reunited.

17

Cransome carefully scooped up Mrs. Spenser in his strong grip, and he and Havenson mounted into flight toward the nightingale's garden.

"Do you see? The dawn is breaking," exclaimed Havenson as they flew above the lumpy darkness of the trees. "It's a new day."

Through an ebony frame of feathers Lorne could see how the pearl-gray sky ahead of them was pregnant with pastel hues. His dreams were coming true. Mrs. Spenser's thoughts, however, from within the friendly cage of Cransome's claw, somehow returned to the lower garden and to all the creatures still confined down there. Her husband had not risked his life to get to the upper garden just to please himself, and neither had she. Was this just a selfish victory?

As if reading her thoughts, Cransome spoke up. "You will both have the feeling that you are coming home when you get there, a feeling of comfort and familiarity. But don't forget that you have a mission. You have important parts to play down in the lower garden. You will take the message of joy back to your friends."

"Yes," Mrs. Spenser chirped. This was as it should be.

"But for now," Cransome called, "we're going home."

And at that moment the sun rose over the top of the hill with a blast and gush of gold. A lark began to trill avidly above them. The dangers and uncertainties of the night had fled away. Even the darkest corners of their hearts—corners they had not known were there—were flooded with a joyous light. All despair was gone, and hope came forth with a mighty shout.

Up they soared above the gently swaying crowns of trees that had begun to smolder as with an inner fire. Havenson hailed a passing hawk, who closed his eyes in the standard sign of respect for a superior.

Could it be possible that they were soaring toward the higher garden? A mighty sense of confidence swelled in Mrs. Spenser's breast, and she wished for a moment that Lieutenant Cransome would let her go so that she could fly by herself to the presence of the nightingale. Indeed, she suddenly felt that she could fly as high and fast as any crow or hawk. But did she look terrible? Her coat of feathers must look soiled and tattered after that night. What would the nightingale think of her? She wished she had some gift to bring, something to give him that would thank him for his beautiful songs that brought such happiness to the inmates of the lower garden.

Lorne dared to peek out as they sailed higher than he had ever gone. Beyond the topmost trees he glimpsed what looked like colored light. Even orange and yellow seemed to glisten there. It was a radiance, an effulgence that grew stronger and stronger as they approached. He, too, yearned to fly free of Cransome's shoulders—to dart and dip and swoop and soar above the deeply glowing trees and arrive under his own power at the precincts of the higher garden. But he clung and gazed, his happy heart brimming full.

As they drew nearer, the light of the dawning sun—or was it some other light?—grew dazzlingly, blindingly bright. Both Lorne and Mrs. Spenser had to look away from time to time and found themselves looking only askance at the great effulgence they approached. A new emotion stirred in their breasts: It was a kind of fear, but majestic and grand. Or perhaps it was awe. Their hearts raced and pounded. Were they too small and weak after all? Would they melt away under the heat that produced the light? Was this, then, death itself?

As they came to the edge of the last trees, a lake glistened beyond like diamonds and opals and emeralds. Something graceful and white moved there. A swan! How blissfully it sailed. A delicious rose-like fragrance enveloped them. The air itself seemed to glisten and sparkle with tiny, nearly invisible diamonds.

As they melted swiftly into the ecstasies of the light and entered the garden, the song of the nightingale came pealing forth. Such triumph in the sound! Such tenderness, such loving-kindness! Such utter warmth of a father's and a mother's welcome, pouring, flooding, surging wave on wave of happy, sparkling life, surrounding them with towering waves of rapturous song in a vast, an infinite embrace.

And then they knew. Lorne knew; Mrs. Spenser knew. Yes—here they could fly.

Sliding off the satiny back, dropping out of the opening claw, Lorne and Mrs. Spenser swooped up to a shelf of air, looked at each other with happy, knowing smiles, and shot like arrows toward the bull's-eye of the light.

They were home.